The
BIGGEST
BEAR

Story and pictures by LYND WARD

A TRUMPET CLUB SPECIAL EDITION

Published by
The Trumpet Club
1540 Broadway
New York, New York 10036

ISBN: 0-440-84202-6

Reprinted by arrangement with Houghton Mifflin Company
Printed in the United States of America
September 1988

10 9 8 7 6

Johnny Orchard lived on the farm farthest up
the valley and closest to the woods.

On the hill behind the barn, Johnny's grand-father had planted a few apple trees. These were the only apple trees in the valley, and they were known as Orchard's orchard.

Whenever Johnny went down the road to the store for a piece of maple sugar or something, he always felt humiliated. The other barns in the valley usually had a bearskin nailed up to dry. But never Johnny's barn.

Every fall for three years Mr. McLean had come in with a bear.

And one evening Mr. Pennell had just stepped out to the edge of his nearest field and shot three in a row as they came heading for the tall timber.

It is true that Johnny's grandfather had met a bear once when he was on the way back from picking apples. But he had gone in one direction, while the bear had gone in another.

When Johnny had asked him why, his grandfather had said, "Better a bear in the orchard than an Orchard in the bear." It was very humiliating.

Johnny said, "If I ever see a bear, I'll shoot him so fast he won't know what hit him. And we'll have the biggest bearskin in the whole valley."

After he had gone quite a way into the woods, he came to a place where there was a big stump. Something seemed to be moving in the bushes behind it!

It was a bear all right.

He seemed hungry, so Johnny gave him a piece of maple sugar.

On the way home, the bear ate all the maple
sugar Johnny had in his pocket.

Johnny's mother and father were a little surprised to see that Johnny had really brought a
bear back with him. Johnny's grandfather said,
"Humph, I suppose you know what a bear likes
to eat."

The bear liked the milk that was meant for the calves.

He liked the mash meant for the chickens.

He liked the apples in the orchard.

He liked pancakes on Sunday morning.

And most especially he liked the maple sugar
Johnny brought him from the store.

There was hardly anything he didn't like, and Johnny's mother got pretty upset when he started looking for things on the kitchen shelves.

In the fall, Mr. McCarroll got pretty upset
when the bear spent a night in his cornfield.

In the winter, the bear had a wonderful time with the bacons and hams in the Pennell's smokehouse.

It was bad enough that he emptied all the sap buckets when the McLeans were tapping their maple trees in the spring.

But it was worse later when he got in the McLean's shed and drank up most of their maple syrup. He was always eating, it seemed, and he grew pretty fast and got pretty big.

Finally Mr. McLean started talking to Mr.
Pennell. They both went to see Mr. McCarroll.
Then they all came to see Johnny and his father.

What they had to say about Johnny's bear
was plenty. He was a trial and a tribulation to
the whole valley.

After the men had left, Johnny's father explained to Johnny that the bear would have to go back to the woods.

So the next morning Johnny and the bear started out. They walked for miles due west, on an old lumber road, way past Baldwin's hill, to an old clearing that was overgrown with raspberries.

Johnny explained to the bear that the time had come for him to go and live in the woods like other bears. He gave the bear a last hug and started the long walk home.

While he was doing the chores next morning, Johnny saw that the bear hadn't stayed in the woods very long.

So Johnny started out again, due east this time, to the blueberry bluff, way past Watson's hill. And when Johnny left him, the bear was eating blueberries very happily.

But two days later he was back again.

This time Johnny took him due south and got a boat and rowed two miles out in the lake and left him on Gull's Island, which is a pretty big island.

But the next morning, there he was, not even very wet.

Johnny and his father talked it over, and they decided there was only one thing to do. Johnny said he would do it.

They didn't really have to go very far, but Johnny somehow kept on walking.

They went north this time. There were no roads here, and it was a part of the woods where Johnny had never been before.

At last they stopped. Johnny seemed to have
a hard time getting a bullet in the gun. While
he was working with it, the bear seemed to get
a whiff of something.

Without warning, he took off through the woods. Johnny went with him.

They went through the woods so fast that Johnny lost his gun. But he held on to the rope. They seemed to be heading for a sort of little log house.

They went through the doorway pretty fast, and something came down with a bang and they were prisoners.

When Johnny looked around, he saw the bear was happily chewing on a big lump of maple sugar that had been put in the trap for bait.

Pretty soon some men came. They were a little surprised to see Johnny in there.

They explained to Johnny that they were getting animals for the zoo in the city. They were delighted with Johnny's bear. He was much bigger than they had ever hoped for.

"He will have a fine place to live, and all he wants to eat," the men told Johnny. "And you can come and see him whenever you want to."

"And I'll always bring him maple sugar," said
Johnny.